T0198775

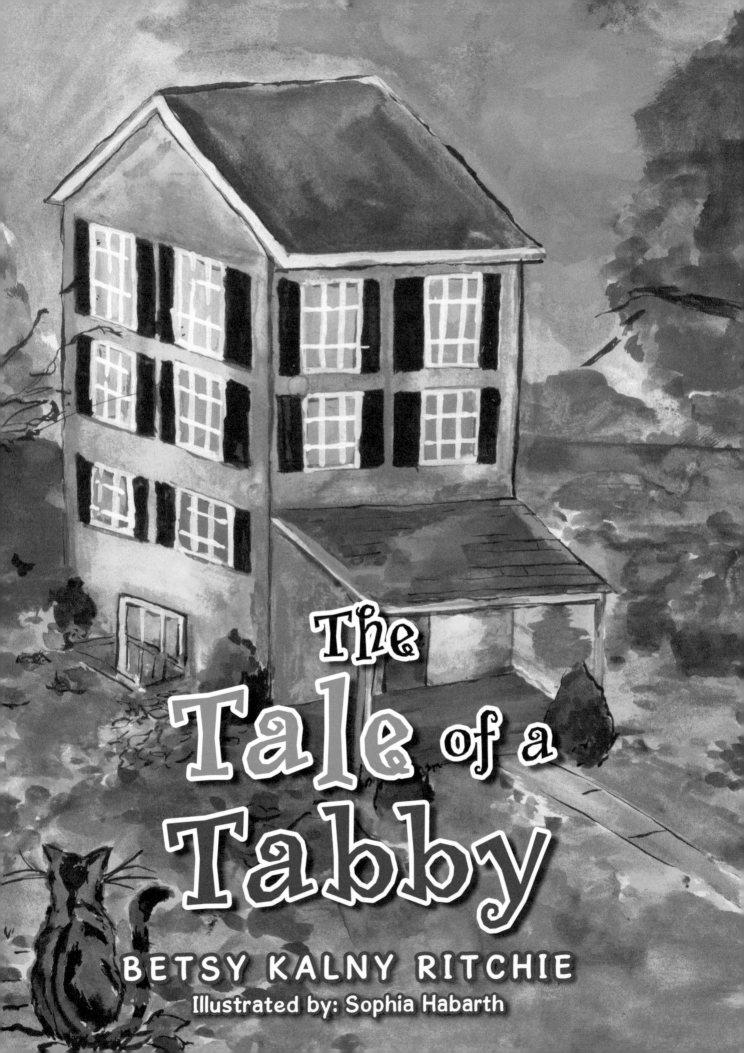

The Tale of a Tabby

BETSY KALNY RITCHIE

Illustrated by: Sophia Habarth

Balboa Press books may be ordered through booksellers or by contacting:

Balboa Press
A Division of Hay House
1663 Liberty Drive
Bloomington, IN 47403
www.balboapress.com
844-682-1282

ISBN: 979-8-7652-3680-2 (sc)
ISBN: 979-8-7652-3681-9 (e)

Print information available on the last page.

Balboa Press rev. date: 11/30/2022

BALBOA.PRESS
A DIVISION OF HAY HOUSE

Foreword

The Tale of a Tabby is a tender story about patience. In this hurried world we sometimes forget the value of being patient with others and even ourselves. Each creature, human being and any other living thing travels a different life journey with different encounters and experiences. All living things, then, may have a different timeline in this journey. Without patience life can be a quick fix or a blur. With patience and understanding one's journey can be richer, more beautiful or very fulfilling.

I want to especially thank my amazing daughter, Brooke, and my dear husband, Don, for their never-ending support in writing this true little story. Thank you to my illustrator, Sophie, who kept her promise. Also, thank you to my late friend, Dave, who suggested my writing this story. Of course, a big thank you to the little brown tabby with the orange nose.

With love,
Betsy

ONE MORE THING PARENTS: *The Tale of a Tabby* has its own glossary in the back page for the underlined words.

This little brown tabby was rescued and fostered by CatNAPS of Pottstown. For each book that is sold a small contribution goes towards CatNAPS of Pottstown.

Once upon a chilly October morning, Mommy-cat was ready to bring new kittens into this world. She was a wise mommy and knew her baby kittens would need a safe, warm home. So, she strolled to the cozy yellow house on High Street. Mommy-cat knew that this house had deep, wide <u>window wells</u>—just the right size to protect her kittens from the cool and windy weather.

Now, the family in the yellow house on High Street were caring people, and they wanted the <u>litter</u> of kittens to be protected. So they allowed Mommy-cat to use their window well as a <u>nursery.</u> With concern for the litter, this caring family in the yellow house called Mrs. B., the lady from the Cat <u>Rescue</u> Company.

1

A few days before Halloween, Mommy-cat's kittens were born. There were six adorable balls of fur! There were two black kittens, two tabby kittens, and two tortoiseshell kittens. Mommy-cat had to feed and clean her six baby kittens. She had many other jobs to do.

Soon, her kittens were quickly growing and roaming. They also needed to learn lessons, such as how to cross the busy streets, how to choose healthy foods, and who or what to trust. They had to learn about the sounds around them, such as the *crunch* of leaves and what that might mean or the *whoosh* of fast-moving cars or even the *thumps* of people's feet on the driveway. So busy was Mommy-cat that she did not teach her kittens <u>manners</u> or how to behave.

One early December day, Mommy-cat and the six kittens—three girls and three boys—walked into town. Mommy-cat was the leader with the kittens lined-up one behind the other. But they did not stay that way. No way! They were roaming here and there and everywhere. Mommy-cat was teaching them to use their noses to smell, their ears to hear sounds, their little legs to run, and their brains to think. Mommy-cat was teaching them very well! But she was not teaching them good manners. There was no time!

As Mommy-cat led her band of kittens to town, the brown <u>tabby</u> kitten used his little orange nose to smell the sweet, buttery scents from Beverly's Pastry Shop. He was very curious about *all* food! He thought, *What is that wonderful smell, and why are we looking for stinky day-old fish?* But Mommy-cat was too busy, and there was no time for sweet and buttery <u>aromas.</u>

Beverly's
PASTRY

GOODIES!
CAKES   CUPCAKES
PIES   COOKIES
MUFFINS PASTRIES

Mommy-cat noticed that her kittens were grown up enough for her to leave them alone in the window well for just a little bit of time. So off she went to hunt for food for her family. While Mommy-cat was in town hunting for scraps, her litter managed to leave their safe nursery and wander in the yard. On that same chilly day, Mrs. B., the cat expert and cat caretaker, <u>observed</u> the litter of kittens from a hidden area near the yellow house on High Street. Mrs. B. thought, *This litter needs to be rescued before winter arrives!* Just then, Mommy-cat was strutting up to the yellow house on High Street with yummy scraps of chicken skin and fish tails for her kittens.

It was now December, and the winter air was cold and wet. "Brrr," said the kittens, shivering. Mommy-cat knew she needed a warmer home and more food for her growing kitten family. The kittens were <u>rascals</u> and wanted to go to town on their own, all by themselves. <u>Curiosity</u> took the kittens in many different directions. The little brown tabby wanted to find sweet scents. The others had interests of their own, such as chasing fall leaves and finding mice. Where would they wander off to? Would they get lost in town? Who could they trust? Did they know how to cross streets in town?

What could Mommy-cat do?

Mommy-cat needed help!

Luckily, on that wintry day in late December, Mrs. B. and her two helpers arrived at the yellow house on High Street to rescue Mommy-cat and her litter from the icy weather. The window well was no longer roomy or warm enough. Mrs. B. and the helpers had saved many stray cats from the harsh, wintry outside world. At first, Mrs. B. and her helpers tried catching Mommy-cat, but no matter how hard they tried, Mommy-cat slipped away every time.

Mommy-cat scurried to a shrub near the yellow house and found a secret spot to hide. She watched closely as Mrs. B. and the helpers gathered the six kittens. Mommy-cat was sad but also glad to know that her kittens will be safer and warmer, with food in their furry, round bellies. But Mommy-cat knew that living in a home was not her lifestyle. Mommy-cat thought, *I'm a <u>stray</u>, and I'll stay that way!* But she knew this would be best for her kittens.

Mrs. B. brought Mommy-cat's lovely litter to her warm home to foster the six wild little kittens. Until then, the kittens had lived outside on the streets in town. During January they needed to learn a lot, including house behaviors and good manners, because in February they were going to find families to stay with forever.

First of all, the kittens did not know humans. They thought, *Should we trust them?*

They weren't used to eating food out of a bowl instead of an old trash can. How did the food get there?

One of the new rules was no scratching or fighting or biting each other or anything or anybody. Yikes!

There was no tree in the house to scratch on; they had a scratching post.

And what was the point of this litterbox thing?

Mrs. B. had to be patient. She knew kittens, especially <u>feral</u> ones. She believed these kitties were smart and able to learn better behavior.

The six kittens were learning lessons and behaving better. But there was still work to be done. The black kitten wandered all around Mrs. B.'s house. The tabby girl was very scared and stayed in her cage. The brown tabby, the one that loved sweets? That little rascal wiggled his nose, stuck it in the air, and followed anything he smelled. *Yum*, he thought. Then he quietly tiptoed with his unusually big paws into Mrs. B.'s kitchen, where he found buttered toast and oven-baked cookies. He knocked over and scattered the chocolate chip cookies on the floor and had a cookie party all by himself! Later he got in BIG trouble with Mrs. B.

Soon February arrived, and it was time for Mrs. B. to take Mommy-cat's lovely litter to the pet store to find their forever homes. She hoped that they would behave very well. As much as Mrs. B. loved cats, she could not keep all that she helped.

On the drive to the pet store, the kittens licked themselves clean in hopes to be chosen to be part of a family forever. Many pet store customers oohed and aahed at the kittens on display.

Into the pet store walked Betsy, a customer and cat volunteer. Betsy and her family were now ready for a new furry family member. Well, to Betsy's surprise, she met the little brown tabby, and it was love at first sight.

When Betsy arrived home, she announced, "The new kitten is here!" The family came running to greet this little rascally tabby who loved baked goodies.

They set up a room for the little brown tabby to get used to the new home. His room had food and water bowls, cat toys, and a litterbox. But he would eat and use the litterbox only when no one was around.

In the evenings Betsy and her daughter, Brooke, would go to the tabby's room and spend time with him. Because the tabby was frightened of his new surroundings, he would stay under the brass bed. So Brooke did homework, and Betsy read a book, hoping he would get used to their scents and their voices. Brooke offered the tabby treats to coax him out. But nothing worked; he stayed under the bed.

On the way to school after five days of the tabby staying under the bed, Betsy said, "Brooke, I don't think we can keep this cat."

"Why?" said Brooke sadly.

Betsy replied, "This little kitty lived outside; then he went to the foster home and is now here. He is too scared to come out from under the bed. Maybe he needs to live on a farm where he would be outdoors or to go back with Mrs. B. I will call her today," said Betsy with disappointment in her voice.

Betsy thought and thought about the little brown tabby and what she should do. Then she called Mrs. B., who was a cat expert. Mrs. B. reminded Betsy that the little brown tabby was a stray and that they needed to give him more time and <u>patience</u>.

During a walk in the neighborhood that evening, the family discussed the tabby kitten and whether they could keep him. The family knew they needed patience. But how many days should the family wait—ten? Fourteen? Twenty?

That night Brooke and Betsy went to the tabby kitten's room planning to spend time coaxing and waiting for the him to appear. But instead...

... the little brown tabby with unusually big paws crept slowly out from underneath the brass bed. He *stretched* and yawned. He even explored some other rooms!

Their patience had paid off. The family agreed that this brown tabby belonged in their home. Yippie! The little brown tabby was even purring.

Finally, thanks to patience, the little brown tabby had a permanent home, the family had a new cat, and the cat had a name: Buster! This is our tale of our tabby, **Buster**.

Colors of Kittens in Mommy-Cat's Litter

Black Cat

Tortoiseshell Cat

Brown Mackerel Tabby

The Tale of a Tabby Glossary

Aroma—a scent, smell, fragrance or odor

Curiosity—the need to know

Feral—wild or not tame animals

Litter—a name of a group of baby animals all born at the same time

Manners—a proper or correct way of behaving or acting

Nursery—a room where babies sleep and are cared for

Observe—to watch and look carefully; pay attention to

Patience—having the ability to wait and not rush

Permanent—staying the same; not changing

Rascal—an animal or person who plays tricks for fun or causes mischief

Rescue—to save and protect from danger

Stray—to wander from the group or path

Tabby—a cat with fur that is striped with brown or black

Window well—an open area near a window around the foundation or base of a home

Printed in the United States
by Baker & Taylor Publisher Services